Neon Snow

LIANA BROOKS

OTHER WORKS

ALL I WANT FOR CHRISTMAS

All I Want For Christmas Is A Reaper
All I Want For Christmas Is A Werewolf

FLEET OF MALIK

Bodies In Motion
Change of Momentum

HEROES AND VILLAINS

Even Villains Fall In Love
Even Villains Go To The Movies
Even Villains Have Interns
Even Villains Play The Hero (books 1 – 3 omnibus)
The Polar Terror

TIME AND SHADOWS

The Day Before
Convergence Point
Decoherence

SHORTER WORKS

Fey Lights
Prime Sensations
Darkness and Good

Find other works by the author at
www.lianabrooks.com

Neon Snow

INKLET #89

LIANA BROOKS

www.inkprintpress.com

Print ISBN: 978-1-922434-29-6
eBook ISBN: 9798201589066

www.inkprintpress.com

National Library of Australia Cataloguing-in-Publication Data
Brooks, Liana 1982 –
Neon Snow
54 p.
ISBN: 978-1-922434-29-6
Inkprint Press, Canberra, Australia
1. Fiction—Fantasy—Urban 2. Fiction—Short Stories

First Print Edition: September 2022
Cover photo © babkin via Deposit Photos
Cover design © Inkprint Press
Interior art © Amy Laurens

NEON SNOW

Snow fell in large, fluffy flakes through the night, drifting between the multicolored Christmas lights and the palm fronds at the edge of the junkyard. Yes, snow when it was eighty degrees out with ninety-nine percent humidity. It was better to think of it as snow than chemical ash from the permastorm that churned over the Gulf of Mexico, spitting hurricanes up and down the Atlantic seaboard.

Don't lick it. Don't touch it. Don't —for the love of all the gods—try to melt the stuff. Let it fall. Sweep it away. Dump it somewhere far from civilization, or at least far from the bits of civilization that have money to pay to get the snow far away from them.

Yalana breathed in, taking in the smell of rancid garbage rotting along the dark street, the brine of the ocean air lapping against the beach, the smoke and spice of the Junkyard. It wasn't as sterile as a city building, nor fetid as the alleys where work sometimes called her. It smelled of death— everything on Earth did these days— but it was a lively, irreverent death that flipped the bird to the satellites overhead and the lunar colonies watching everyone down here who was still waiting for rescue.

A flake of snow came uncomfortably close to her face. Yalana blew it away, hunched her shoulders, and flipped the collar of her camel-colored coat up. Long sleeves, long pants in a darker brown, heavy brown combat boots hidden under the slacks. With a little luck, the only thing she'd burn tonight was time and the goodwill of the Coast Guard commander, who was probably just realizing that she hadn't left the port to cruise around the open water with her lover.

The Junkyard was under quarantine; it had been most her life. It was one of those festering sores of modern living that polite society liked to forget existed. A little town on the Florida panhandle that had continually voted to tax the poor rather than the rich and support land grabs over addressing the rising sea levels.

The rich left when the tide got high. Everyone else, the ones who thought they were one lucky break away from being rich enough to leave, were either dead or somewhere in this half-floating park of madness.

Houses on stilts and houseboats were tied together by weak ropes and anchored to the pieces of mud the storms hadn't yet washed away. It was only a matter of time before the Junkyard was another set of flotsam battering the sea walls protecting Tallahassee.

The people here didn't care.

They came because they didn't want to go to rehab for whatever vice they loved so much. Or maybe because they'd stopped loving everything and wanted to die in a party.

Music and uneasy laughter rolled out of the windows. Everything was for sale in the Junkyard. Everyone had a price.

It was a good place to get lost.

And a good place to hunt for lost souls.

The mud path from the port had once been lined with wood, but most of it had washed away. Now the land underfoot was changing, growing dryer with each step, rising upwards into a small hillock crowned by chain link fences with wood and steel debris lashed to them.

Fist-sized lightbulbs in every color imaginable were strung along the top of the fence, dancing gently in the tropical air.

Two large sections of gate were propped open by heavy barrels of burning driftwood. Blue and purple flames crawled skyward, singeing the snow and giving off a choking smoke that caught the light in odd ways.

A man stepped out of the shadows, wiping large hands on a dirty, yellow cloth. He wore a ripped black vest and faded, gray pants too large for him, held up by a heavy black belt. His eyes were dark and far more focused than any Junkyard denizen was expected to be.

He cocked his head, the light filling in more colors. Purple hair tied up in a knot—and just the knot; the rest of his head was shaved. The rest of him looked hairless too, probably a sign of snow poisoning. It leeched in like that, slowly killing off the outer layers of the body until the skin was little more than scar tissue. In the city it was treatable. Out here...

...She'd worn a coat for a reason.

"You look like you're a long way from home," the man said in a low drawl with hints of New Orleans and Atlanta.

"I am." Yalana put her bare hands in her pockets. "Ever heard of Quebec? It's north of here."

The man's eyebrows—what was left of them—went up and fell with little sign of recognition. "North is as far as the moon."

"Hmm. Well then. You know north where the Yankees live? I was born north of that north."

"I know about Canada." He smirked. "What I don't know is what a pretty little snow bunny is doing playing down here with the sharks." He turned and his vest opened enough to show the black ink outline of a shark with tribal knots.

"Since when was this Shark territory? Word was this belonged to Shiftly."

The man shook his head. "Sorry, beautiful. Shiftly's shuffled off."

Dead. Two-week-old intel was the best money could buy and it still wasn't enough.

"You looking for trouble in general?" the man asked. "Or just the kind Shiftly sold?"

"I'm looking for something special." It was doubtful the man could see her smile in the dark, and even less likely that he'd understand why she was smiling, but she smiled anyway.

"Special costs extra." He made a point to turn and look her up and down. "You got money. We like money here."

"I'll pay with anything but my body. The rest"—she opened her arms—"you can have it. I'll walk out of here naked if it gets me what I want."

He sauntered closer. In the firelight his face was carved and hard. Dangerous. Lethal. "What is so special you're risking your skin for it, beautiful?"

"My lover." She pulled the picture of grinning man from her pocket. In the photo he still had youthful, chubby cheeks, even if his fair hair was receding. "I'll pay anything to get him back."

"Anything?" The man with the purple hair and the shark on his side took the picture. "For him?"

"Yes."

For a minute the Junkyard dog didn't seem like he believed her. "His life means that much to you?"

"It means everything to me."

"You'd give up everything for him?"

"Except my own life. Yes. My body isn't for sale."

The man turned the photograph over in his hands.

Snow fell silently between them.

Yalana's lips twitched up in a cold smile. "You've seen him."

The man shrugged in acknowledgment. "This man. Beautiful, you don't want him."

"I do."

"He's..." The man shook his head. "His head's not right."

"I want him for his body, not his brain."

That earned her a skeptical look. "His body?"

"Yes."

The man turned, fully displaying hard muscles and island-tanned skin. Whether he'd been born with dark gold skin or simply spent too much time in the sun was impossible to tell in this light. His features were an amalgam of every nation that had fought over this blood-soaked sand bar in the past seven centuries. "You're hurting my ego, beautiful."

"I'm sure your ego will survive the night."

He tapped the photograph again. "I know how you can find him."

"Name the price."

"No haggling?"

"I don't need to haggle. I can pay or I can walk."

The man's smile chilled the hot night air. "Give me his last kiss."

"You want to kiss Jackson? Fine."

The man shook his head. "No, not the last kiss from him. The last kiss for him, from you. I want the kiss you want to give your lover before he dies."

The intel hadn't included anything about kissing. It was right on the border of her comfort zone, but not an impossible line to cross, merely unpleasant. She'd suffered through much worse over the years.

"Isn't your lover worth a kiss?"

"Are you clean?" Yalana asked.

"Clean as a whistle," the man promised.

"Clean as a whistle on the sand of a dirty playground covered in snow." There were antibiotic shots on the boat though. It would probably be enough. "Fine. I kiss you and you give me Jackson."

"Ah. No. You give me your last kiss for this man. One final kiss for your love, and then you may never, ever kiss him again."

The tension in her shoulders eased. "If I do?"

"He'll die," the man said simply.

"You'll watch? You'll know? That seems unlikely."

The man shrugged. "Call it superstition."

"Whatever. A kiss for Jackson. That's the trade. No touching. No extras. Just mouths. No blood."

"Come here." His voice was seductive.

She raised an eyebrow. "The trade is for a kiss. I won't come when you call. You want payment, come here." She put her hands back in her pockets, fingers stroking the smooth handle of her gun.

"You are a very angry kitten." He stepped toward her, hands held out to either side but not reaching for her.

Yalana kept her expression bored. If the man was looking for a reaction from her, he wasn't going to get one.

He was larger up close. Taller. Broader. Far more captivating. "It has to be a real kiss," he warned. "I'll know if you're thinking of your lover or not."

"You're a mind reader now?" She almost smiled for real.

"I have many talents."

"Prove it." She closed her eyes and focused, not on Jackson, but on the dream of love. Moonlight on water. A house in the swamps surrounded by water and lightning bugs. Laughter. Her lover's lips on her neck. Warm arms embracing her.

Lips—real lips—touched hers, soft and commanding. For a moment she was in the dream, the smell of wood smoke and her lover's soap curling around her. A tongue stroking hers, promising a night filled with delights.

A kiss that left her glowing with anticipation was replaced by a cold absence.

She opened her eyes and found herself face to face with the stranger.

Dark eyes held hers, emotions flashing like strange fish through stormy seas. "You'll never have that with Jackson again. Never. If you kiss him, if you try to take back what you gave, his life is forfeit."

"I kiss you and get the magic kiss of death?" Yalana raised an eyebrow. "Don't promise me things like that. I might become a repeat client."

"I know what you felt. Your dream of a house in the quiet, under a clear sky."

"Keep talking like that and you're going to have recruiters knocking on your door. The military loves people who are more than what they seem."

The man smirked. "I don't take orders from anyone."

"Then we have something in common." And she'd won the first round. "How do I find Jackson?"

"You'll have to follow me." Round two to the stranger. He turned away quietly, walking through the gates towards a log house on stilts with the same garbage patch decoration as the fence.

Yalana studied it and shook her head. "What did you do, paint the house with glue before the last hurricane and catch whatever came your way?"

"It helps," the man said.

Helped with what, was the question. But not one she had time to pay for. If she wasn't back to the dock before dawn, she'd have larger problems than the ones already threatening to destroy everything around her.

The house was dark. Not a surprise. The Junkyard wasn't exactly on any city's grid. Glass hurricane lamps with oil sat on windowsills unlit. The lanterns outside gave an illusion of light, but not enough to see more than ominous shadows.

"Here." The man stopped in the middle of the darkness. There was a scratching sound, glass against wood, and then a small orb of glowing blue liquid was shoved towards her. "Not as good as the surveillance in a city, but it will glow brighter as you get closer to him."

Yalana shook it, watching the liquid inside as it jumped and swirled. "Interesting. What's it made out of?"

"Stuff."

"What happens if I break the bottle?"

"Don't."

"Worried about losing a lucrative trade secret?"

"Worried the stuff smells like rancid potatoes and it burns your eyes worse than snow. And it evaporates fast. Breaking the bottle isn't worth your time. Remember what happens to curious kittens."

"Curiosity killed the cat, but ingenuity brought it back."

"That's not how the saying goes."

It was for her. "If I can't find Jackson, I'll be back."

"You want your kiss back?"

"No. I'll take repayment in blood. Kitty cats eat fish, didn't you know?"

Leaving the building was easy, all she did was follow the light. By the time she reached what was laughably called the town square, the orb in her hand was glowing brightly enough to illuminate the muddy path in front of her.

She tested it, walking east and then west, watching the glow to see if it was actually reacting to her movements or only growing because the chemicals inside the glass were growing brighter.

It glowed brightest as she walked north by north-east, toward the smell of smoke and the sound of drums.

People fell out of the shadows, approaching her and then veering away when they saw the orb. The Shark Man must have had more influence than he let on.

Bottles. Glass. Chemicals. Sobriety.

He was probably supplying drugs of one kind or another. Medicine was expensive, even if a person had a city job. Here in the Junkyard there would be no state-funded medical supplies. The man wouldn't be the first to leave a life of rigid laws to enjoy the hedonistic pleasures that medical skills could bring.

He'd demanded a kiss from her just for a bottle. What was he asking from others?

The thought twisted her gut. *Should have shot him when I had the chance.* Predators like that could never be reformed.

An overly thin woman wearing a ripped, green dress and lanky hair with snow burns broke away from the nearest cluster of community to approach Yalana. "Who are you?"

"I'm looking for Jackson." Yalana took another photograph out of her pocket.

"You saw the doctor?"

"If that's what you call the man on the hill, yes."

The woman shivered. "It was a bad trade."

"What did the man on the hill do to you?" There was time enough to drag Jackson away from this pit stain of a place and shoot the man on the hill before dawn.

"Nothing. He did nothing." The thin woman shrugged. "But, your man." She touched the photograph. "He's dying. He's lying there, sweating, dying. Sick. He's sick. No one can make him better."

Yalana didn't try to hide her relief. "He's breathing. That's all that matters. Show me where he is. I'll pay you. Food rations. Medicine. Whatever you want."

The woman rubbed at her arm.

"Clothes?" Yalana guessed. "I have more."

"Bottled water?" The woman's eyes were wide with hope.

"I'll give you a case if you show me where Jackson is and walk us to the docks."

Eagerly the woman sprinted ahead into the crowds.

Yalana followed, not quite running—because these weren't the kind of people who took well to sudden changes—but keeping pace and following to a rickety shack under a huddle of blackened palm trees. There was a ladder of sorts rather than stairs. She took the rungs two at a time and pushed away the blanket hanging between the walls, the only protection from the snow outside.

The air smelled sour. Rotting flesh and fermenting fluids had never been so welcome.

"Jackson?"

There was a wheezing breath from a dark corner.

Yalana held up the orb.

Jackson lay on the floor, clothes ripped and skin bloody from scratching. His eyes were half-open and he was too dehydrated to sweat.

"You're alive." She smiled.

"He's dying," the other woman said.

"He's been dying for weeks." Yalana looked around for a way to carry Jackson. "Everyone else died within seventy-two hours of contracting the virus. But Jackson is alive. And there's no one else sick on Junkyard. Do you know what that means?"

The woman shook her head.

"It means he found a vaccine of some kind. A way to slow the virus." But there was nothing to carry him with.

Yalana tore the blanket away and rushed back to the party outside.

The purple-haired man stood there, casually talking with someone. Watching her with sharp eyes.

She ignored him. "I need four or five strong people to carry a man for me."

Someone in the crowd snickered.

"Free passage to the mainland for anyone who helps me. No border check. No questions asked."

"You think your boat's still there?" a woman's voice scoffed.

Yalana smiled. "My boat is waiting and there's a Coast Guard cutter standing guard. I need a man carried. Now. free passage to the mainland. This might be the last offer anyone makes in a while." She turned and marched back to the hut.

The sound of several people hurrying along behind her made it clear that someone had listened. There were five in all. Two women who looked older than they probably were. Three men who looked barely out of their teens, if they were at all.

"This man is sick but not contagious," Yalana said. "Lift him, carry him to my boat, and you can all come with me. Or you can take the supplies I brought in case I needed to stay. Water. Clothes. Medicine. Addiction treatments. Radios. I have everything you could need."

She stepped back and let them reach for Jackson. He moaned in distress, and it was the most beautiful sound she'd heard in weeks.

Their odd party cut through the edge of the Junkyard, following the curve of the land down to the port.

As the stranger at the party had predicted, there were people waiting, trying to access her boat. The ripple field was keeping them back for now. It wasn't a strong electric current, but strong enough to shock them and none of them were inebriated enough to walk through the moment of pain to reach the boat.

Yalana went in front of her people carrying Jackson. If the thieves needed somewhere to focus, then she'd be the one in the spotlight. She whistled, sharply, the sound cutting through the background noise. "Hello."

"Hello." The largest one had a heavy coat that had maybe, once upon a time, been blue or gray. Now it was an indistinct shadow of a color, but it was protection against the snow. "You're a pretty little fish, aren't you?"

"What do you want?" Yalana asked.

The lead man looked her up and down. Under the yellow dock light his skin was yellow. Swollen. With sores on his face. This specimen wasn't nearly as clean as the shark she'd tangled with earlier. "I want everything, pretty girl. Give that to me, and I let you live."

"No trade. Move aside."

The man stepped closer. "The trade is good. I like a—"

Yalana squeezed the trigger. There was a small hole in her coat pocket, not big, and not ideal for targeting, but she'd practiced with it for years. Rarely had a need to use this gun with actual bullets, but the shot went straight.

The man fell dead on the dock.

"No trade," Yalana repeated. "Anyone else have an offer?"

The mob who'd come with Yellow stared at her. One of them moved fast, grabbed her arm.

"Remove your hand," Yalana ordered.

He leered at her.

Yalana brushed her thumb across the heavy ring on her free hand, felt the slight click as it transformed from a large, domed gem to a much spikier weapon, and punched. She cut into the men's neck and dragged her hand down. The wounds weren't deep, but they'd burn.

The would-be boat thief lost his grip and stumbled to his knees.

A boot to the face and he toppled into the filth-choked water of the port.

"No trade," she repeated.

The remaining thieves scattered.

Clicking her ring back in place, Yalana glanced over her shoulder. Her pack of new followers had been joined by the Shark Man. She raised an eyebrow at him. "Problems?"

"Angry little kitty cat."

"Kittens have claws. People should remember that." A wave of her hand and the ripple field fell. "All aboard, who's going. And a case of water for the thin woman."

The Shark Man stepped closer, almost crowding Yalana, but giving her enough room to sidestep if she wanted.

She didn't. "You had your trade. I told you I'd pay anything. Give you anything."

His eyes caressed her face like he was trying to burn the memory of her into his mind. "I made the right trade. But you... Won't you regret giving up the lover you're willing to kill for?"

"No." Unequivocally and without question.

Lightning flittered overhead, jumping between the clouds in the ever-present maelstrom.

In the storm's light, it almost seemed like the man's eyes glowed. "You will be back."

"Perhaps. But not for you."

"No?" He smiled as if he'd heard a joke. "You left your heart dancing in the moonlight. It's here now."

"Good for my heart. I've never used it before and I'll never need it in the future. Enjoy using it for whatever you think that kiss magically gave you.

Everyone deserves to have dreams of moonlight without snow."

The man frowned. "Do you believe you're heartless already?"

"Check my pulse." She grabbed his hand and pulled two fingers to her neck. "Feel anything?" She waited as her boarding party loaded Jackson onto the boat. "Anything? No. There's nothing there." She dropped the man's hand. "I was born heartless."

"There's more to a heart than the beat of blood. There's love."

"Never had that either." Yalana stepped aboard the boat and pulled the rope loose from the mooring. "Any other cryptic messages for me before I leave?"

The man looked at the party of refugees hurrying to hide from the snow as the wind picked up. "Take care of them."

"I will."

"I'll see you when you get home."

"Not unless you have a much better boat than I do."

"Home is where the heart is."

She laughed. "Then I'll see you at home, in the darkness."

Let him keep her heart. She had what she needed now to create the vaccine, and her search was at an end.

THE MAKING OF
NEON SNOW

I had a dream of warm snow at a Miami beach party.

The winter holidays in warm places are always a little strange to me: you have all the holiday decorations but none of the traditional snow and cold. It is, by far, my favorite way to spend a December holiday.

I played with the idea after I woke, setting up a vaguely post-apocalyptic world, but it never became something real. For now, it's this and only this. A mysterious smile, a willingly given kiss, and a future filled with darkness and warm snow.

Read more by Liana Brooks!

The late Dr. Everett's Many-World inter-pretation of quantum mechanics is notable for two reasons. One, it is laughably simple. Two, it is almost correct. Had Dr. Everett recalled that there is no particle without a wave, our research would now be an exercise in tedium. Alas, it is the failing of generations past that they did not consider the wave form and thus anticipate the eventual collapse of iterations not held stable by Pointer States, or ein-selection nodes.

~ Excerpt from Lectures on the Move-ment of Time *by Dr. Abdul Emir I1–20740413*

Friday May 17, 2069
Alabama District 3
Commonwealth of North America

With an asthmatic wheeze, the engine died. It figured. Stuck in a man's craw, it did. This truck had been his daddy's and his pappy's, and before the Commonwealth government forced him to replace the diesel engine with the newfangled water doo-hickey, he was certain he'd pass the truck on to his son.

He'd been playing under the hood of trucks since he was six, and now he was stranded. Embarrassing, that's what it was. He climbed out of the cab to check the engine out of habit. The ice-blue block of modern fuel efficiency stared back. Three hundred bucks it'd cost him, straight from his pocket.

Oh, there was a government subsidy, all right. A priority list. Major population centers, they said. Unite the countries of the Commonwealth on a timeline, they said. And what did all that mean?

It meant the damn Yankees got upgraded cities and free cars before the ink was dry on the Constitution, and what about the little man? Nobody thought about the working class. No one cared about a man covered in oil and grease anymore.

He thumbed his cell phone on.

No reception. Figured.

So much for the era of new prosperity.

He'd hoof it. There was a little town

about five miles down the road where he could call Ricky to bring a tow truck. It would have been cheaper to pay the diesel fines than get all this fixed.

Off schedule. Over budget. Son of a—

He stared at the distant oaks. Well, it wasn't going to get any cooler.

He grabbed his wallet and keys from the cab of his truck. The tree line looked like a good spot to answer a call from nature, then he'd see if there was a shortcut through to town.

A meadowlark sang. Not a bad day for a hike. Would've been better if it weren't so dammed hot, but at least the humidity was low. He wouldn't like to walk in a summer monsoon, not at his age, with arthritis playing up.

Under a sprawling pine tree, he unzipped his pants. As an afterthought, he glanced down to make sure he wouldn't stir up a hill of fire ants.

A hand lay next to his boots.

He blinked, zipped his pants slowly, and turned around. "Hello?"

Cicadas chirped in answer.

"Are you drunk?"

The quiet field that had looked so peaceful only moments before was now eerily sinister. He nudged the hand with his foot. It was swollen and pale and crusted with blood, just like a prop out of a horror movie.

Maybe it was a good idea to *run* to the next town.

They say a coward dies a thousand deaths, a brave man only one. Where underpaid, overstressed probationary agents fell in that spectrum, Sam wasn't sure, but she'd bet her last dollar she was headed down the slippery slope of a thousand cowardly deaths. Any sensible person would not have picked up their work phone after eight on a Friday night, or at least would have the spine to tell their boss they weren't going to work on the weekend.

Which was exactly what Senior Agent Marrins wanted Sam to do.

On a curving old road between two towns untouched by a century of change, in a place where streetlights were still considered new technology, some broke-down trucker had found a body. Three miles west, and it would have been someone else's problem. In any other district, it would have been the senior agent's problem, and she would have tagged along to get the work experience needed for promotion.

Sam didn't work in any other district, though. She worked in Senior Agent Marrins'. Which was why she was driving out to this rural stretch of road.

The wash of the Milky Way glittering overhead was beautiful, if you were into that sort of thing. Sam would have preferred the gaudy show of lights in any major city in any major first-world country. "Saint Jude, pray for me who am so miserable," she whispered as the crime scene came into view. Three police cars, an eighteen-wheeler, and an ambulance... Not your typical Friday night in Alabama District 3.

An unfamiliar police officer knocked on the window and made a circular motion. "Ma'am, this is a crime scene. I'm going to ask you to keep moving."

"Officer, I'm Agent Samantha Rose from the Commonwealth Bureau of Investigation, and I'm going to ask you who the hell you think would drive out this far from civilization at this time of night."

He blinked at her.

"Precisely. Would you please step away from my car and call the officer in charge? Thanks." Men. They weren't all idiots, but she'd seen little evidence that these illiterate hicks could prove it.

"Rose?"

Sam closed her car door and looked around. "Detective Altin?" A man who towered a full foot over her should not have been able to hide.

"Behind you."

She spun and almost tripped into the older man. "I thought you were going to the movies with your wife."

"She took the kids instead. Twenty-five years married to the force, she'll forgive me." Altin's teeth flashed as he grinned. "You just won me a bet. The sergeant from Cherokee County was certain Marrins would come out himself."

"Has the sergeant *met* Agent Marrins?" Sam asked. "The only time that man hustles is when there's a fresh box of donuts at the secretary's desk." She shrugged. "I live on this side of the district. Marrins wrote this off as effective delegation of resources."

"I thought Marrins would at least try to get this on his resume. The last time we had a homicide where there were actual questions was that horror-house case that hit all the national news stations, and that was over a decade ago. Isn't that how the bureau promotes?" Altin's grin widened.

Sam rolled her eyes. "Yeah, but a dumped clone isn't a homicide investigation. It's littering."

"Who said it was a clone?"

"Agent Marrins."

"He's psychic now?" The detective raised a skeptical eyebrow.

"He said the police called him about a dumped clone, and I needed to sort it out."

Altin shook his head. "I wouldn't jump to conclusions. People might be eager to dump their clones before the Caye Law goes into effect and they have to pay a tax on them. But there are organ-donation stations that take the clones for free. No one's going to drive all the way out here to chop up a clone and dump it. Too much work."

"There are still reasons why someone

might skip the legal methods of disposal." Like having an illegal clone. Her first case fresh out of the academy in Langley had been busting an illegal-clone ring using stolen DNA to sell fetish slaves to stalkers. Rows of growth-accelerated children who went from infant to adolescent in under a week, half-starved and chained to the walls of the California mansion's attic.

Their vacant stares still haunted her dreams.

She crossed herself out of habit, then pulled on her forensic gloves. "Okay—let's go meet Jane Doe."

Keep reading! Head to
www.inkprintpress.com/
lianabrooks/timeshadows/
daybefore/
to buy your copy now!

ABOUT THE AUTHOR

LIANA BROOKS loves the beach at night, though possibly not with toxic snow drifting down from on high.

By day, Liana enjoys writing science fiction in every form, from sprawling space operas romances (the *Fleet of Malik* series) to the antics of a super-powered family (the *Heroes and Villains* series).

Liana also maintains a soft spot for paranormal romances. She writes the popular *All I Want For Christmas* novellas, including *All I Want For Christmas Is A Werewolf* and *All I Want For Christmas Is A Reaper*.

You can learn more about her and her books at www.LianaBrooks.com.

INKLETS

Collect them all! Released on the 1st and 15th of each month.

Dancer, Dreamer
Seer
LIANA BROOKS

As Time
Whirls Slowly
Past
AMY LAURENS

Far More
Satisfying
Than Hell
AMY LAURENS

Just
Another Day
In Hell
LIANA BROOKS

Moon AND
Morning
AMY LAURENS

Some
Impropriety
Expected
AMY LAURENS

NEON SNOW
LIANA BROOKS

Reincarnation
LIANA BROOKS

More Than
Mushrooms
AMY LAURENS

DOUBLE ISSUE
INKLET #092
How To Make A Star
& The World Ended
LIANA BROOKS

INKLET #093
CAUGHT
IN THE ACT
AMY LAURENS

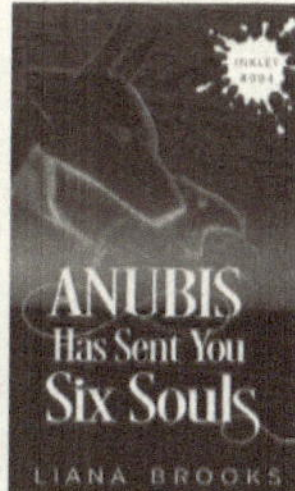

INKLET #094
ANUBIS
Has Sent You
Six Souls
LIANA BROOKS

INKLET #095
PRAYER TO A
GODDESS
LIANA BROOKS

INKLET #096
Love In The
Time Of Corona
AMY LAURENS

INKLET #097
RECRUITMENT
AMY LAURENS

INKLET #098
IDENTITY
Theft 101
LIANA BROOKS

INKLET #099
Curses
With Benefits
AMY LAURENS

INKLET #100
NECROMANCER
TROUBLES
LIANA BROOKS